THE LAST SUPPER
A MUSICAL ENACTMENT

MUSIC BY
GARY WILLIAM FRIEDMAN

BOOK AND LYRICS BY
THOMAS MITZ

BASED ON AN ORIGINAL CONCEPT BY
ANDY KREY

ARRANGEMENTS AND ORCHESTRATIONS BY
GARY WILLIAM FRIEDMAN

SAMUEL FRENCH
FOUNDED 1830
NEW YORK HOLLYWOOD LONDON TORONTO
SAMUELFRENCH.COM

IMPORTANT BILLING AND CREDIT REQUIREMENTS

All producers of THE LAST SUPPER *must* give credit to the Author of the Work in all programs distributed in connection with performances of the Work, and in all instances in which the title of the Work appears for the purposes of advertising, publicizing or otherwise exploiting a production thereof, including, without limitation, programs, souvenir books and playbills. The names of the Author(s) must appear on a separate line in which no other matter appears, immediately following the title of the Work, and *must* be in size of type not less than 50% of the size used for the title of the Work.

Billing *must* be substantially as follows:

(NAME OF PRODUCER)

Presents
(100%)
THE LAST SUPPER
A Musical Enactment

(50%)
Music by
Gary William Friedman

Book and Lyrics by
Thomas Mitz

(25%)
Based on an Original Idea by
Andy Krey

Arrangements and Orchestrations by
Gary William Friedman

When Song Selection appears in Program, an asterisk (*) *must* appear by the song "You Are the Light" to indicate: Lyrics by Thomas Mitz and Stevie Holland.

****

The Score (music and lyrics) to *THE LAST SUPPER*
is published by 150 Music.
www.150music.com

CHARACTERS
(In order of appearance)

THE CHOIR
LEONARDO
THE ANGEL
PETER
PHILIP
BARTHOLOMEW
LITTLE JAMES
MATTHEW
JOHN
MARY
MARTHA
SIMON
THADDEUS
PRIOR
ANDREW
JUDAS
JAMES
THOMAS
JESUS

SETTING

Dinning Hall of the Monastery Santa Maria Delle Grazie, 1497,
and the imagination of Leonardo

PRODUCTION NOTES

THE LAST SUPPER is easy to produce. It is accessible to both professional and amateur performers and church groups in particular. It is not necessary to cast singing actors. The singing is done by a choir and soloists who perform a function similar to a Greek Chorus by expressing the meaning and emotion of the action through song, and the spoken text, primarily monologues, is delivered by actors. The exceptions to this are Jesus, who sings and speaks, and the Angel, a woman who steps out of the choir. The show can be performed in a theater, a church, or in practically any space. The only indispensable prop is the table at which the final tableau takes place. Simple toga-like costumes add much to the production and can be copied from a reproduction of Leonardo's painting. The choir can be dressed in robes, formal wear or simple black. There should be something about the Angel that sets her apart. Ideally, for the representation of the full spectrum of the score, the choir would consist of three sopranos, three altos, three tenors and three baritones but any combination or number of singers will work. If need be, the entire score could be performed by one soloist. A piano is needed; bass and flute parts are also available.

COMPOSER'S INTRODUCTION

Very little of what I'd been doing in the theatre prepared me for the incredibly unique and 'religious' experience I had while working on the composition and subsequent productions of THE LAST SUPPER.

It began on a day in the fall of 1998 when Thomas Mitz called to tell me that he'd been commissioned to write the libretto and lyrics for a show about how Leonardo Da Vinci came to paint the mural depicting Jesus and his disciples at what was to be forever known as *The Last Supper*.

Knowing that I was not a Christian, he asked with some trepidation if I'd be interested in composing the music for the show.

The question I asked myself was: could I, a composer who is Jewish, create music for a production so firmly rooted in an event so deeply meaningful to Christians? I searched my conscience to seek some kind of answer that could enable me to become a part of the endeavor.

I thought that insofar as *The Last Supper* depicted a Passover Seder led by Jesus, who was a Rabbi, it would be in keeping to have the Jesus character sing and speak in Hebrew. This insight somehow gave me the confidence to proceed. I could now be true to Christian history as well as to my Jewish roots.

The theatrical 'modus' of the show is to humanize the Apostles, each of whom comes forward as if right out of the imagination of Leonardo to express his fears and joys at the prospect of devoting his entire life and being to following this Rabbi, a man whom all sense was in imminent danger.

Each (spoken) statement by an Apostle is characterized and commented upon by the Choir which sings in a highly charged emotional and inspirational manner—a kind of hip Greek Chorus.

As the first production in New York got underway, it was apparent that yet another character needed to be introduced and developed—a character who would serve as an inspirational muse for Leonardo. Thus the Angel was "born," and having the luxury of my wife Stevie Holland nearby, I proceeded to create musical numbers around her extraordinary voice and presence.

The climax of the show occurs when Jesus appears at the Passover table and begins to chant the Hebrew prayer *Sh'ma Yisrael* as well as the Blessing (in Hebrew) over the bread and wine. When He exclaims: "One of you will betray me!," all the Apostles freeze and become a tableau of Leonardo's *Last Supper*.

The Chorus then sings the *Sh'ma* in English translation—that is, The Lord, Our God Is One!...and to a thundering **AMEN** the show ends.

May it go on to inspire, enlighten and entertain forever.

Gary William Friedman

*(A basic black stage. PLATFORMS, Stage Left or Stage Right, for
CHOIR to stand on. A large WHITE FLAT, 16 feet, along back
wall, Center Stage to Stage Right. A TABLE, 14 feet long, in front
of WHITE FLAT. Seating (BENCH or STOOLS) for 13 between
table and WHITE FLAT.*

The CHOIR enters and takes its place on stage.)

SONG: OVERTURE

CHOIR.
TREACHERY!
BETRAYAL!
AND LOVE AND FEAR
AND FAITH AND DOUBT
AND HOPE AND DEEP DESPAIR,
AND SCHEMES AND GREED AND WHAT WE NEED—
ALL THIS WITH YOU WE SHARE.

A MAN WITH MANY GIFTS
ABANDONED HIS IDEAL.
ANOTHER MAN WAS VILIFIED
FOR TRUTHS HE DARED REVEAL.
DESERTED BY HIS FRIENDS HE DIED,
BETRAYED AT THEIR LAST MEAL.

WHERE IS OUR FAITH?
ONCE IT WAS STRONG.
WHERE IS THE LOVE
THAT HELD US TOGETHER SO LONG?
HAS IT LEFT US FOREVER?

WHO WILL DECEIVE?
WHO HAS THEIR PRICE?
WHO RUNS AWAY?
WHO MAKES THE GREAT SACRIFICE?
WILL ANYONE REMEMBER?
SO COME AND JOIN WITH US

AND ENTER IN OUR FOLD.
A FADED PAINTING ON A WALL
HOLDS SECRETS AGES OLD.
SEEK WITHIN AND YOU SHALL FIND
A STORY TO BE TOLD.

(LEONARDO enters. He is a man with long hair, dressed in stylish fifteenth century clothing.)

LEONARDO. I've looked down into the mouth of hell many times. It's always paralyzing. My personal vision of hell is not one of agonized bodies writhing in pain. Satan, that supreme ironist, has made my hell white — a pure field of white — like a blank piece of paper. Or like this wall. *(LEONARDO rises and turns his back to the audience. LIGHTS UP on WHITE FLAT.)* For sheer terror, nothing compares with a blank surface. At one time in my life it spurred me into action, confident of victory. I drew from a bottomless well of inspiration. Today the blank surface sets off a different reaction — fear of failure and humiliation, guilt. It has been ten years since my last painting — a portrait of one of the Duke of Milan's empty-headed paramours. Despite such a negligible subject I created a majestic portrait of breathtaking beauty integrated with a magnificent background combining nature and antiquity, expressing the deepest principles governing the cosmos. Unfortunately, someone pointed out to the socially ambitious beauty that a cracked vase in the painting represented her loss of virtue. She complained to the Duke and the Duke had the entire background painted black. Pearls commissioned by swine. Why bother to paint when a painter is regarded as nothing more than a tradesman? A decorator. Which is precisely why I had left Florence and entered the Duke's service to begin with. Florence — a city overrun with painters — scores of them, begging for commissions by day and filling the taverns by night — dirty, paint splattered — drinking, bragging, back stabbing, whoring — nearly as bad as sculptors. This was Leonardo? Not if I could help it! When I wrote to the Duke of Milan, offering my services, I described myself as an inventor, an engineer, a man capable of making machines of war, casting cannon and creating equestrian statues. Only at the very end did I mention that I was also a painter. Having a gift for painting served me well in the beginning. I was born the illegitimate son of a Florentine notary — not an auspicious beginning. When I was eight years old, I painted a dragon on the door of our house that sent my father running in terror when he came to visit his mistress, my mother, thus proving that art can have a function. Soon after that I was sent away — apprenticed to the master painter Andrea del Verochio — and it wasn't long before I was painting all but the finishing touches of his commissions. When I was fourteen he let me paint an angel in a major work. I used no model. I could see the angel as clearly as if she were sitting in front of me.

(The ANGEL appears.)

LEONARDO. *(continued)* Even as a boy my mind would formulate wonderful plans — plans that would bring me honor and glory and wealth far beyond those of a painter. I would become so exalted that the disgrace of my birth would be obliterated. And so it seemed to happen. The Duke accepted the offer of my services. Glory was within my reach. I came to court adorned in velvet. I was received with the respect I had longed for. And what happened? Promises, made with the greatest enthusiasm, were never kept. Military designs that inspired awe where never financed, my inventions the subject of ridicule. My function? To play the lute and decorate the garden. So I'm back where I started. I am to paint this dining hall in the Monastery Santa Maria Delle Grazie with a depiction of the Last Supper so the fat monks have something to gaze upon while they stuff their faces. Here is my hell — the white surface — to be faced alone.

SONG: VISIONS

ANGEL.
YOU ARE NEVER ALONE, LEONARDO.

LEONARDO. *(Spoken)* I used to be able to summon inspiration at will.

ANGEL.
WHEN YOUR PROBLEMS ARE GREAT

LEONARDO. I just don't know what to do.

ANGEL.
FIRST YOU MUST ASK,

LEONARDO. Dear God, tell me what to do.

ANGEL.
THEN YOU MUST WAIT.

A VISION CAME TO ME,
A REVERIE OF HARMONY,
A BEAUTY I COULD NEVER
LIVE WITHOUT.

BUT VISIONS FADE AWAY
WITHOUT THE FAITH TO MAKE THEM STAY,
SO QUICKLY DISAPPEARING
INTO DOUBT.

THE WORLD ALL AROUND US
IS MERELY A FAÇADE
THE VISIONS THAT SURROUND US
ARE GLIMPSES OF GOD.

OH VISIONS, COME TO ME,
WITH OPEN EYES LET ME SEE
THE BEAUTY AND THE MEANING
OF LIFE AGAIN.

*(LEONARDO has changed gears, his creative mind begins to work.
MUSIC UNDERSCORED.)*

LEONARDO. A moment frozen in time. The moment at the Last Supper when Jesus tells the disciples, "One of you will betray me." Who were these men? How did they react? It was Passover. One week after Jesus' triumphant entrance into Jerusalem when the masses threw palms in his path and welcomed him as the chosen one. Just days earlier he had shocked his disciples by using violence to throw the money changers out of the Temple. Crowds of people listened to him every day and followed him wherever he went. And among those crowds were spies and informers. Jesus wished to spend Passover with his disciples and he gave them instructions to find the secret room for the meal. The disciples must have been overflowing with excitement. For three years they had given up their former lives, their possessions, their families to follow one man. All they owned was faith. They knew the hour of destiny was near. After this Passover meal nothing would ever be the same again. I must try and understand what led each one of them to this table.

CHOIR.
THE WORLD ALL AROUND US
IS MERELY A FAÇADE.
THE VISIONS THAT SURROUND US
ARE GLIMPSES OF GOD.

ANGEL.
OH VISIONS, COME TO ME.
WITH OPEN EYES LET ME SEE
THE BEAUTY AND THE MEANING
OF LIFE AGAIN,
THE BEAUTY AND THE MEANING OF LIFE.

(LIGHTS FADE on LEONARDO as he goes to wing Stage Right. He sits unobtrusively and draws. LIGHTS UP as PETER enters. We see each DISCIPLE enter as he is named by PETER and take his place on stage.)

PETER. I've got two swords hidden under my cloak, two short Roman stabbing swords, double-edged, sharp as a razor. If I knew who the traitor was I'd shove one of them between his ribs right now, even if it were my brother Andrew. But it's not him. I never trusted that Zealot, Simon; he's a political revolutionary at heart. He's for Jesus if he thinks Jesus is for the cause. And Thaddeus was mixed up with that lot too. The Romans could have something on him. Or Matthew, once a tax collector, always a tax collector and he hasn't collected any tax in a long time. On the road to Jerusalem James and his pretty boy brother John were arguing about which one of them would sit on Jesus' right hand. Jesus put them in their place but good, right in front of everybody. John is close to the Master and James has a fool's courage, it could be either one, or both. Bartholomew and his friend Philip deserted John the Baptist for Jesus, who's to say they wouldn't desert Jesus for someone else? Judas gets messages from his family claiming he left them starving and begging for money, and Thomas — never trust a man who thinks too much, especially if you can't understand what he's talking about half the time. And Little James, the small quiet one nobody notices, just biding his time, that's the type you have to look out for. Whoever the traitor is hasn't reckoned on Peter being here, or these swords of mine. I'll never leave his side. Anyone who tries to lay a hand on him is dead. And that goes for anyone who doesn't do the right thing and defend him. Maybe I shouldn't have drunk so much Passover wine — I haven't had wine or meat in a year. No, I'm glad I did. Otherwise I might show mercy on the traitor. I'm ready.

SONG: STAND LIKE A ROCK

CHOIR.
HOW CAN THIS ANGER STAY LOCKED UP INSIDE?
I DON'T KNOW HOW I CAN KEEP IT FROM BREAKING OUT NOW.

SOLO.
HOW LONG WILL IT TAKE ME TO SEE
ANYONE CAN TELL YOU A LIE?
NO MATTER HOW THEY TRY,
OR WHAT THEY GUARANTEE,
YOU NEVER KNOW ON WHOM TO RELY.

CHOIR.
THINK ABOUT A PLAN TO SURVIVE.
FIND MYSELF A WAY TO BE STRONG.
I'M NOT THE ONE WHO'S WRONG.
I'LL KEEP MY PLAN ALIVE
AND FIGHT THEM IF THEY DON'T GO ALONG.

SOLO.
I'LL NEVER BEND.
LIKE A BLOCK
OF SOLID ROCK
I'LL STAND UNTIL THE END.

CHOIR.
I'LL NEVER RUN.
HERE TO STAY,
I WON'T BETRAY
THE WORK THAT I'VE BEGUN.

SOLO.
LOOKS LIKE I WILL HAVE TO ARRANGE
TO SHOW THEM WHAT A ROCK I CAN BE.

CHOIR.
THE PRESSURE'S NOW ON ME
TO TRY AND MAKE A CHANGE,
TO TRY AND TEACH THE BLIND TO SEE.

SOLO.
I'LL NEVER HIDE.
SHOW NO FEAR
WITH DANGER NEAR

CHOIR.
AND TAKE IT IN MY STRIDE.

STAND LIKE A ROCK.
DON'T ADMIT
WHEN I'VE BEEN HIT.
REFUSE TO LET IT SHOW.

SOLO.
I'LL NEVER BEND.
LIKE A BLOCK
OF SOLID ROCK
I'LL STAND UNTIL THE END.

CHOIR.
I'LL NEVER RUN.
HERE TO STAY
I WON'T BETRAY
THE WORK THAT I'VE BEGUN.

STAND LIKE A ROCK
DON'T ADMIT
WHEN YOU'VE BEEN HIT.
TAKE EACH BLOW,
DON'T LET IT SHOW,
REFUSE TO QUIT,
REFUSE TO GO.
STAND LIKE A ROCK.

(PHILIP and BARTHOLOMEW move downstage.)

PHILIP. Bartholomew and I grew up together. I was a little older, a little bigger, and, naturally, the leader.
BARTHOLOMEW. When we played soldier I had to be the Roman.
PHILIP and BARTHOLOMEW. *(in unison)* We were best friends.
PHILIP. When I heard about the wild man prophet John com-

ing out of the wilderness to preach and baptize, I got Bartholomew and told him — We're going. Together we listened to his call to repentance and the coming of the Messiah. Our hearts burned with hope, our childhood games were about to become reality.

BARTHOLOMEW. All Philip could talk about was John the Baptizer. Then one day Philip comes up to me so excited I could barely understand him.

PHILIP. I've found him! I've found him!

BARTHOLOMEW. Who would that be, my friend?

PHILIP. Who do you think? The one Moses and the Prophets wrote about — the one John the Baptizer has been telling us about — the ONE — Jesus of Nazareth!

BARTHOLOMEW. *(to audience)* Right.

PHILIP. He thought it was funny.

BARTHOLOMEW. It wasn't the name Jesus that struck me — I had never heard of him — but the association of our long-awaited Messiah with the name Nazareth — a dirt-poor hovel of a village known for nothing but ignorance and hostility to strangers. *(to Philip)* You can't be serious. What good thing could come out of Nazareth?

PHILIP. Come and see. *(to audience)* I took Bartholomew to Jesus. There was a group of people, many of whom we knew, listening to him.

BARTHOLOMEW. When I approached, Jesus stopped talking and looked at me. "Look," he said to those around him. "an Israelite with no evil in his heart." I felt a little flustered by this sudden attention. How do you know? I asked him. "I've been expecting you. Before Philip brought you here I saw you under the fig tree." What is he talking about? I thought. This was my first exposure to Jesus' habit of telling the truth by talking in circles. Then I understood. In our country, working mothers shelter their babies from the sun under the shade of fig trees while they are in the fields. Just by looking at me he knew who I was, where I came from, what I was looking for. My heart was filled with a joy I had never known before. Suddenly nothing else was important anymore. "Rabbi," I said, bowing my head.

PHILIP. That was nearly three years ago. He saw the future then. Does he see it now?

(PHILIP and BARTHOLOMEW clasp each other on the shoulder.)

SONG: GOD HAS A PLAN FOR ME

SOLO.
LIKE THE ROAR OF THE MIGHTY WATERS,
LIKE THE THUNDER OF THE SEA,
I'M BURSTING WITH THE GOOD NEWS:
GOD HAS A PLAN FOR ME.

LIKE THE END OF THE BITTER WINTER,
LIKE THE FIRST BUDS ON THE TREE,
I FEEL MY LIFE BEGINNING.
GOD HAS PLAN FOR ME.

LIFT UP YOUR SPIRITS.
CAST OFF YOUR GLOOM.
HOPE HAS BEEN PLANTED,
SOON IT WILL BLOOM.

CHOIR.
SUNLIGHT IS SPREADING.
WAKE UP AND SEE.
GOD HAS HIS OWN PLAN
FOR YOU AND FOR ME.

I USED TO THINK I WAS ALONE,
A LEAF THAT BLEW ACROSS THE SAND.
NOW I KNOW I'M PART OF SOMETHING GRAND.

SUNLIGHT IS SPREADING.
WAKE UP AND SEE.
GOD HAS HIS OWN PLAN
FOR YOU AND FOR ME.

SOLO.
LIKE THE SIGHT OF A FRIENDLY HARBOR
TO THE HOMEBOUND REFUGEE,
MY RESTLESS SEARCH IS OVER,
GOD HAS A PLAN FOR ME.

CHOIR.
LIFT UP YOUR SPIRITS,
CAST OFF YOUR GLOOM.
HOPE HAS BEEN PLANTED,

SOON IT WILL BLOOM.

SUNLIGHT IS SPREADING
WAKE UP AND SEE.
GOD HAS HIS OWN PLAN
FOR YOU AND FOR ME.
GOD HAS A PLAN FOR YOU AND —
GOD HAS A PLAN FOR YOU AND —
GOD HAS A PLAN FOR YOU AND ME.
GOD HAS A PLAN.

(LITTLE JAMES and MATHEW move downstage.)

LITTLE JAMES. I'm the least worthy to be here. The least significant. I'm not even the first disciple named James. It was "Little James" from the start. I've always been the face in the crowd.

MATTHEW. Lesson one — people with money despise and trample on those without. Deal with it. My first loyalty, before God, before my nation, before my neighbors, before my own pride was to my family. I did what I had to do to save us from starvation without becoming a criminal.

LITTLE JAMES. When John was baptizing and stirring the hearts and minds of all who listened, I was one among many. I looked into the faces of those around me. I saw the look of hope and excitement that I was feeling. Soon we would be free of the warfare, misery and oppression we lived with. I first learned of Jesus in a conversation I overheard. They weren't talking to me, but I couldn't help but eavesdrop. I followed them at a distance.

MATTHEW. Those of us who collected taxes were hated by everyone. Even the Romans we worked for despised us. I kept a percentage of what I collected. I was doing my duty to my family. All this I told myself when I was shunned by everyone and treated as an outcast by my own people. All but one. A Holy Man. A blessed rabbi.

LITTLE JAMES. They led me to him. I listened. What I heard brought peace to my soul. I followed him, going wherever he went. There were many of us who followed him, with more and more joining each day. I was grateful no one paid much attention to me because if they did I was sure they would question my qualifications and ask me to leave.

MATTHEW. Others crossed the street when they saw me. He came to me, this man respected by all, and said, "Follow me." And I followed. I wanted to express my gratitude and offered to prepare a feast for him and his disciples. To my surprise he consented and asked that I invite my friends.

LITTLE JAMES. Then one day he went to the top of a mountain by himself. We all waited for him through the night. Everyone knew something important was going to happen, but we didn't know what. Some slept; I couldn't. I wrapped my cloak around me, leaned up against a tree and thought about my life. I knew I would have to go back to my old life sooner or later. That made me very sad but then I realized I should be grateful for what had happened to me. I had seen the Master with my own eyes and heard him speak with my own ears. If that's all there was, that was enough.

MATHEW. Friends? Did he know what he was saying? I couldn't think of one respectable person who would even speak to me voluntarily. I confessed to the Master the only people who would associate with me were other tax collectors and some soldiers who provided enforcement for us. He told me to invite them. I did and he welcomed them with love.

LITTLE JAMES. When he came down from the mountain the next morning he announced that twelve of us would be his apostles. I was curious to see who he would choose. When he looked in my eyes and called my name I was thunderstruck. I had never met his gaze before. I didn't know he even knew my name, there were so many of us.

MATHEW. When Jesus was publicly denounced for sitting at my table I felt such shame. But he felt none. "Those who are well have no need of a physician but those who are sick do," was his response.

LITTLE JAMES. The love and gratitude I felt overwhelmed me.

MATHEW. My old self died and a new one was born. Now the others suspect me. They know my background. Please let the man I was remain dead.

SONG: HOW DEEP IS YOUR GAZE

SOLO 1.
WHAT DID YOU SEE IN ME
THAT NOBODY ELSE COULD SEE?
WHAT WAS IT THAT REVEALED
THE HOPE THAT I KEPT CONCEALED?

CHOIR.
HOW DEEP IS YOUR GAZE THAT PENETRATES.
HOW STRONG IS YOUR LOVE THAT EMANATES.

HOW KIND IS THE HEART THAT STOPPED TO SEE
WHAT NOBODY ELSE COULD SEE IN ME.

HOW DEEP IS YOUR MIND THAT UNDERSTANDS.
HOW STRONG IS THE TOUCH WITHIN YOUR HANDS.
HOW KIND IS THE MAN WHO LOOKED TO SEE
WHAT NOBODY ELSE COULD SEE IN ME.

    SOLO 2.
THE WORLD SAW ME AS LESS THAN DUST,
A BROKEN TOOL THAT TURNED TO RUST.

    SOLO 3
YOU SAW ME WITH DIFFERENT EYES —
EYES THAT SEEMED TO UNDERSTAND
AND NOT DESPISE.

    CHOIR.
HOW DEEP IS YOUR GAZE THAT PENETRATES.
HOW STRONG IS YOUR LOVE THAT EMANATES.
HOW KIND IS THE MAN WHO LOOKED TO SEE
WHAT NOBODY ELSE COULD SEE —
WHAT NOBODY ELSE COULD SEE —

    SOLO 1.
IN ME.

(JOHN moves downstage.)

JOHN. People forget he is human, he becomes hungry, tired. But hunger, fatigue, stress are all put aside when he is needed. And he is always needed.

(MARY enters.)

MARY. People expect him to be at their beck and call, and he is — out of love. I've never seen him deny anyone to take time to rest. He seeks solitude only for prayer and meditation. My greatest joy is to sit at his feet and listen to him.

(MARTHA enters with broom.)

MARTHA. And while everybody is talk, talk, talking, laying around doing nothing, who do you think has to do all the work? Me! That's who! Do you think one of this crowd of men would lift a finger to help? Not in this world! Miracles! I'll tell you what a miracle is — that the food gets cooked, the clothes washed, the house kept clean.

JOHN. I was grateful when the sisters invited us into their home. Jesus was exhausted and needed to rest. When Martha lost her temper I tried to talk to her. *(to MARTHA)* Woman, you can't talk like that around the Master. Don't you know who he is? *(to AUDIENCE)* She pushed right past me!

MARTHA. I told him, Lord, don't you care that my sister has left me to do all the work? Tell her to help me.

MARY. He smiled at my sister and said, "Martha, Martha, so many things distract you. But you only need one thing."

JOHN. I'm grateful to walk beside him . . .

MARY. . . . to let him change my life . . .

MARTHA. . . . to follow him, to provide what help I can.

(JOHN goes to table. MARY and MARTHA exit.)

SONG: ALL I CAN DO IS LOVE YOU

SOLO 1.
ALL I CAN DO IS LOVE YOU.
ALL OF MY THOUGHTS ARE OF YOU.
ALL I CAN FEEL IS THANKFUL
KNOWING YOU LOVE ME TOO.

SOLO 2.
I NEVER HAD A PURPOSE.
ALL THAT I OWNED WAS WORTHLESS.
LIFE WAS A POINTLESS CIRCUS
BEFORE.

YOU ARE THE WORLD I LIVE IN.
ALL I CAN DO IS GIVE IN.

SOLO 1 and SOLO 2.
ALL I CAN DO IS LOVE YOU
STILL MORE.
ALL I CAN DO IS LOVE YOU.
ALL I CAN DO IS LOVE YOU.
ALL I CAN DO IS LOVE YOU.

STILL MORE.

    CHOIR.
I NEVER HAD A PURPOSE.
ALL THAT I OWNED WAS WORTHLESS.
LIFE WAS A POINTLESS CIRCUS
BEFORE.

YOU ARE THE WORLD I LIVE IN.
ALL I CAN DO IS GIVE IN.
ALL I CAN DO IS LOVE YOU
STILL MORE.

ALL I CAN DO IS LOVE YOU.
ALL I CAN DO IS LOVE YOU.

    SOLO 2.
ALL I CAN DO IS LOVE YOU ——

I NEVER HAD A PURPOSE.
ALL THAT I OWNED WAS WORTHLESS.
LIFE WAS A POINTLESS CIRCUS
BEFORE.

    CHOIR.
YOU ARE THE WORLD I LIVE IN.
ALL I CAN DO IS GIVE IN.
ALL I CAN DO IS LOVE YOU
STILL MORE.

ALL I CAN DO IS LOVE YOU.
ALL I CAN DO IS LOVE YOU.

    SOLO 2.
ALL I CAN DO IS LOVE YOU,
LOVE YOU,
STILL MORE.
    SOLO 1.
ALL I CAN DO IS LOVE YOU.

(SIMON and THADDEUS move downstage.)

    SIMON. Look at them, the sidelong glances, the outright staring the whispering — they think it's me. They're sure I'm the one who will betray him. And God forgive me, I've thought of it.

THADDEUS. All my life I have been concerned with healing but I never possessed the means to become a physician. Then I heard of Jesus and his miraculous powers. It was Simon the Zealot who brought me to him.

SIMON. They still never use my name but call me the Zealot. I believed that armed insurrection against Rome was the only solution and unlike the fishermen who do nothing but talk I put my life on the line. I've ambushed Roman patrols. I've used a sword. I know what it's like to strike and draw blood and I know what it's like to be wounded. I've seen dead comrades and I've taken the enemy's life.

THADDEUS. When Simon and his friends were injured in their violent clashes with the Romans it was I who would hide them and care for their wounds. I knew I would be crucified if I was caught but that didn't matter — a person who needs help is still a child of God no matter how he received his injury.

SIMON. When I first came to Jesus it was because I hoped he was our Messiah and King and would use his divine power to drive the Romans out of our land and establish his new kingdom.

THADDEUS. Simon remembered me when he became a follower. I used to believe that the power to heal was in the physician but I have learned that the power to heal belongs to God.

SIMON. It didn't take me long to realize that the kingdom he talked about was not of this world. He wasn't going to do a damn thing about the Romans. It was then that I thought of betraying him — he was misleading the people, giving them false hope. But he looked into my eyes. He read my thoughts. I knew he was going to expose me, cast me out, maybe have me killed. But he didn't. He embraced me.

THADDEUS. But who is to heal the Master now? Surely God could relieve him of his burden if only he would ask. Surely the betrayer could be healed before it is too late.

SIMON. I deserved death but was given life. I knew I could never pick up the sword again.

SONG: HOW BEAUTIFUL UPON THE MOUNTAIN

CHOIR.
HOW BEAUTIFUL UPON THE MOUNTAIN
ARE THE FEET OF THE MESSENGER.
HOW WONDERFUL THE WORDS HE EXCLAIMS.

SOLO 1.
HOW BEAUTIFUL UPON THE MOUNTAIN
ARE THE FEET OF THE MESSENGER.
HOW WONDERFUL THE WORDS HE EXCLAIMS.

CHOIR.
WHO CAN LIVE IN FEAR?
WHO CAN LIVE IN FLAMES?
THE PROMISED DAY
ONCE FAR AWAY
IS HERE.

NO MORE DREAMING,
NO MORE PAST,

SOLO 2.
TOMORROW IS HERE AT LAST.

SOLO 1.
HOW BEAUTIFUL UPON THE MOUNTAIN

CHOIR.
ARE THE FEET OF THE MESSENGER.
HOW WONDERFUL THE WORDS HE EXCLAIMS.

WHO CAN LIVE IN FEAR?
WHO CAN LIVE IN FLAMES?
THE PROMISED DAY
ONCE FAR AWAY
IS HERE.

NO MORE DREAMING,
NO MORE PAST.

SOLO 2.
TOMORROW IS HERE AT LAST.

CHOIR.
HOW BEAUTIFUL UPON THE MOUNTAIN
ARE THE FEET OF THE MESSENGER.
HOW WONDERFUL THE WORDS HE EXCLAIMS.
HOW WONDERFUL THE WORDS HE EXCLAIMS!

(We see LEONARDO writing in his notebook, lost in creative thought. The PRIOR, the head of the Monastery Santa Maria Delle Grazie, enters.)

PRIOR. Did I wake you?

LEONARDO. You interrupted me.

PRIOR. Impossible. To be interrupted you must be doing something. My workmen have prepared the wall and installed the scaffolding. I already have the bill for your unholy alchemist's brew of paints, and you haven't so much as lifted a brush.

LEONARDO. Prior, men of genius do not need to exert themselves physically to accomplish great things. This phenomenon is called thinking.

PRIOR. I'm not about to be taken in by some glorified loafer who takes money for work that is never completed. I know all about you and how you operate. But you're in Milan now. In my monastery. Beware, painter!

(PRIOR exits. LEONARDO knows there is truth in the Prior's accusation. He holds out his hands and looks at them.)

LEONARDO. Dear God, for all their skill, these hands can never perfectly express what I see in my mind. What is the point of trying?

(The ANGEL enters. She begins to sing.)

SONG: YOU ARE THE LIGHT

ANGEL.
OH LORD, YOU ARE THE LIGHT
GUIDE ME THROUGH THE NIGHT.
LORD, TO YOU I PRAY.
YOU GAVE THE PROMISE TO LIGHT THE WAY.
CREATION HAS OPENED ITS PERFECT DESIGN
AND GAVE YOU THE POWER TO SEE THE DIVINE.
GOD IS THE POWER, HE IS PERFECTION
THROUGH YOU HIS LIGHT WILL SHINE.

THE GLIMMER OF MORNING INFUSES THE SKY.
DEEP IN REFLECTION YOUR LIFE PASSES BY.
TAKE EVERY MOMENT, EACH INSPIRATION
FEELING ALIVE, HOPE SOARING HIGH!

DON'T LET THE PROMISE DIE.

OH LORD, YOU ARE THE LIGHT
GUIDE ME THROUGH THE NIGHT.
LORD, TO YOU I PRAY.
YOU GAVE THE PROMISE TO LIGHT THE WAY.

YOU ARE MY LIGHT,
SHOW ME THE WAY.
ONLY FOR THIS I PRAY.

(ANDREW and JUDAS move downstage.)

ANDREW. This is the greatest crisis. Something must be done. We must close the inner circle around Jesus. Philip, Peter, James, John, Bartholomew too. The six of us lived and worked together in Galilee. We left our homes and families and nets and boats to follow him.

JUDAS. Betrayal? Interesting word. What exactly does it mean? Doesn't being loyal to one person mean that you're being disloyal to someone else?

ANDREW. Not that it couldn't be one of us. No one of us would betray the Master intentionally, but inadvertently? It's possible. Peter has a big mouth. James' lack of physical fear gets him in situations a thinking man would never get into.

JUDAS. If a man pledges before God to support his wife and children and deserts them to follow a dream, isn't he being disloyal, even traitorous to them. Doesn't God's law tell us to honor our parents? Does this mean leaving them destitute and in disgrace in their old age?

ANDREW. By six of us surrounding him, never leaving him for a second, we could protect him from the others, and from ourselves too since we could keep and eye on each other.

JUDAS. Is a man being loyal to the God of Israel when every representative of his God on earth declares Jesus a heretic? Does not God choose his representatives?

ANDREW. We must get out of Jerusalem, back into the country-side, preferably back north. The sheer numbers of people here make it unsafe. A crowd cheering you one second can turn into a mob stoning you the next.

JUDAS. Isn't it ironic then that I, the man who betrayed all those who love him and are dependent on him and threw his lot in with a heretic, am then betrayed by the very man I followed?

ANDREW. The whole city is crawling with spies: high priest's spies, Herod's spies, Pilate's spies, the Zealot's spies. Anyone fighting for power could consider Jesus to be competition and decide he would be better dead than alive. The city is full of pilgrims and he is more popular than ever. This very popularity makes him unsafe.

JUDAS. He told us to be nonviolent and then we watched him thrash honest merchants with a whip. He told us the Kingdom of God was within and then we watched as he let himself be worshipped by crowds throwing palms in front of him while he rode by. We swore ourselves to poverty and gave away everything to the poor and then watched as he let a woman spend a fortune to anoint his feet.

ANDREW. We must protect him now! This moment before it's too late.

JUDAS. I'm not the betrayer — he betrayed me — he tricked me into abandoning my wife, my family, my religion. Now he thinks he's a god. If he is a god, he doesn't need me. He can save himself. He'll find it's not so easy.

ANDREW. Dear Lord, what has happened to us? Where is the love that held us together?

SONG: WHEN IT WAS EASY

CHOIR.
HOLD ON TIGHTLY WHILE WE'RE TOSSED.
IF YOU LOSE FAITH ALL IS LOST.

SOLO.
LOOKING BACK IT'S HARD TO SEE
JUST EXACTLY WHAT WENT WRONG.
IT LOOKED LIKE WE WERE WINNING
WHEN IT WAS EASY.

EVERYBODY SHOULD AGREE
THAT WHATEVER HAPPENS NOW
WE MADE A GREAT BEGINNING
WHEN IT WAS EASY.

WHEN IT WAS EASY TO LOVE
TRAGEDY WOULD NEVER SHAKE US,
POVERTY WOULD NEVER MAKE US AFRAID.
WHEN IT WAS EASY TO LOVE
NOTHING EVER COULD DIVIDE US,
THE ANGER BUILDING UP INSIDE US WOULD FADE.

CHOIR.
HOLD ON TIGHTLY WHILE WE'RE TOSSED.
IF WE LOSE FAITH ALL IS LOST.

SOLO.
IF WE ARE WILLING TO LOVE,
TO LOSE OUR PRIDE AND NEVER MISS IT,
WE'LL GATHER UP THE HURT AND KISS IT GOODBYE.
IT'S NOT SO EASY TO LOVE,
I CAN'T DENY.
IF YOU ARE WILLING TO LOVE
THEN SO AM I.

(JAMES and THOMAS move downstage.)

JAMES. I'm a fisherman. My friends Peter and his brother, Andrew, and my own brother John are fisherman. It can be hard work. It can be boring work. When men fish together they talk. You get to know each other well. We talk about our lives, our problems, our hopes.

THOMAS. Unlike my simple brethren, whom I love dearly, I'm not a fisherman, or a reformed official, or a converted revolutionary. I'm a scholar, a philosopher. I define myself as a combination Skeptic and Stoic, much as Jesus himself, although he only smiles when I suggest as much to him.

JAMES. People tell me I don't think enough. But what's to think about? I say follow your instincts — you can size up a person or situation in the first minute — everything else is a pile of dung. When Jesus came to my brother and me and told us to follow him I didn't hesitate. There are times to think and times to just do it. I nodded to John and we left our boats with our father and his hired hands and never looked back.

THOMAS. Jesus chose me because I can communicate with him on an intellectual level in a way the others cannot. When I consider his final choice of twelve apostles out of all the candidates I admit I am in awe of his judgment. He has assembled a group that can, collectively, reach out to every stratum of society. And out of this group I alone am aware of the many levels of meaning in his teaching. His simplest parables merit deep contemplation. The deepest secrets and abstruse mysteries dwell within his words. And now I am at a loss as to explain his behavior.

JAMES. I knew what my job was — to follow where he would lead me and to tell as many people along the way as I could. We have told the people, first in the North and now here. We traveled unarmed, through territory filled with gangs of bandits, bands of Zealots taking what they need in God's name and bands of Romans taking what they want in Caesar's name and never, never did I experience doubt or fear. Many of the people from the North have come to Jerusalem for the Passover and word of Jesus has spread like a brush fire. And now, for the first time, I am afraid.

(MUSIC BEGINS; UNDERSCORE)

THOMAS. What of this betrayal? I know that when he speaks of his Kingdom he refers to the kingdom within our spirits. So why, two days ago, did he suddenly turn political, attacking every symbol of authority? His actions lead to speculation of his establishing an earthly domain. For that he could be crucified.

JAMES. He told us that fear is lack of faith. I swear I don't lack faith in him, so why am I afraid? He has changed since coming here. I don't question him but I don't understand him either. He always looks directly into people's eyes, seeing right into their souls. When he spoke at the synagogue two days ago, attacking his most loyal followers, he looked as if he were staring at something miles away.

(JESUS enters. HE greets the DISCIPLES one by one. Various VOICES from the CHOIR are heard.)

VOICE 1. Jesus, you promised us a new kingdom — where is it?

VOICE 2. Jesus, you are going to lead us — to where? To death and destruction!

VOICE 3. False prophet!

VOICE 4. Broken promises!

VOICE 5. Evil magician!

VOICE 6. Fake!

VOICE 7. Liar!

VOICE 8. Heal yourself!

VOICE 9. Agitator!

VOICE 10. Traitor.

VOICE 11. Coward!

VOICE 12. Run away!

SONG: DIDN'T YOU KNOW?

CHOIR.
TREACHERY!
BETRAYAL!
IS IT I?
IS IT I?
IS IT I?

SOLO.
I HELD OUT MY HAND TO YOU.
YOU PRETENDED THAT YOU DIDN'T SEE.
MY ARMS WERE EXTENDED
AND WHAT DID YOU DO?
YOU TOOK HOPE AWAY FROM ME
AND REJECTED WHAT I HAD TO GIVE
AND I'M LEFT UNDEFENDED FROM YOUR MOCKERY.
THIS FIRE THAT BURNS ALL DAY,
THIS FIRE THAT FILLS MY NIGHT,
THIS FIRE WILL OUTLIVE
ALL THE HURT,
ALL THE FEAR,
THAT COMES MY WAY.

DIDN'T YOU KNOW?
DIDN'T YOU CARE?
AND IF YOU KNEW
HOW MUCH I CARE FOR YOU
WHY DISREGARD ME?
HOW COULD YOU DARE?

SOON YOU WILL KNOW,
SOON YOU WILL CARE,
AND WHEN YOU DO
I WILL BE THERE FOR YOU.
IN THAT SWEET MOMENT
I'LL HOLD OUT MY HAND.

CHOIR.
YOU TOOK HOPE AWAY FROM ME.
AND REJECTED WHAT I HAD TO GIVE
AND I'M LEFT UNDEFENDED FROM YOUR MOCKERY.

SOLO.
THIS FIRE THAT BURNS ALL DAY,
THIS FIRE THAT FILLS MY NIGHT,
THIS FIRE WILL OUTLIVE
ALL THE HURT,
ALL THE FEAR,
THAT COMES MY WAY.

DIDN'T YOU KNOW
HOW MUCH I CARE?
WHY DID YOU GO?
HOW COULD YOU DARE?
SOON YOU WILL KNOW.
SOON YOU WILL CARE.
AND WHEN YOU DO
I WILL BE THERE.

(The DISCIPLES and JESUS are seated at the table. MARY and MARTHA finish preparing the table. LEONARDO is back on stage. The ANGEL appears.)

SONG: FINALE

ANGEL.
WHAT DO YOU SEE, LEONARDO?

LEONARDO. *(Spoken)* Confusion, pieces to a puzzle but no solution.

ANGEL.
WHERE IS THE VISION YOU'RE SEARCHING FOR?

LEONARDO. I can't see it.

ANGEL.
WHERE ARE THE GIFTS YOU'VE BEEN GIVEN?

LEONARDO. They're gone. My powers are gone.

ANGEL.
WHY HAVE THEY GONE AWAY?

LEONARDO. I am the betrayer!

ANGEL.
DON'T BE AFRAID, LEONARDO.

LEONARDO. It's too late.

ANGEL.
LOOK FOR THE VISION YOU NEED ONCE MORE.

LEONARDO. I have squandered my gifts.

ANGEL.
KNOW THAT YOU WILL BE FORGIVEN.
YOU MAY FIND THE WAY.

LEONARDO. Lord, light of all beings, illuminate my way.

*(CHORUS UNDERSCORES. JESUS and the DISCIPLES enact the
Last Supper as LEONARDO and the ANGEL watch.)*

ANGEL.
THE CANDLES ARE LIT,
THE TABLE IS SET,
FOOD IS ABOUT TO BE SERVED,
SACRED TRADITIONS OBSERVED.
AFTER THIS NIGHT,
DIF'RENT FROM ALL,
NOTHING WILL BE AS BEFORE.
WE'LL BE TOGETHER NO MORE.

(JESUS stands.)

JESUS.
SH'MA YISRAEL
AH-DO-NIGH E-LO-HAY-NO
AH-DO-NIGH ECHAD.

CHOIR.
SH'MA YISRAEL
AH-DO-NIGH E-LO-HAY-NO
AH-DO-NIGH ECHAD.

LEONARDO. They began the Passover meal. He took the bread
and blessed it.
JESUS. Ba-ruch ah-tah ah-doh-nigh e-lo-hay-noo meh-lech haw-

oh-lum ha-mo-tzi leh-chum min-a-haw-retz. This is my body broken for you.

 LEONARDO. Then he raised up a cup of wine and blessed it.

 JESUS. Ba-ruch ah-tah ah-do-nigh e-lo-hay-noo meh-lech haw-oh-lum b'ray p'ree ha-gaw-fen. This is my blood that is poured out for many for the forgiveness of sins.

 ANGEL.
WHERE IS OUR FAITH?
ONCE IT WAS STRONG.
WHERE IS THE LOVE?
THAT HELD US TOGETHER SO LONG?
HAS IT LEFT US FOREVER?

 CHOIR.
WHO WILL BETRAY?
WHO HAS THEIR PRICE?
WHO RUNS AWAY?
WHO MAKES THE GREAT SACRIFICE?
WILL ANYONE REMEMBER?

SH'MA YISREAL
AH-DO-NIGH EL-LO-HAY-NO
AH-DO-NIGH E-CHAD

THE LORD OUR GOD,
THE LORD OUR GOD
IS ONE.
THE LORD OUR GOD,
THE LORD OUR GOD . . .

 JESUS. One of you shall betray me.

(JESUS and the DISCIPLES freeze into a TABLEAU of "The Last Supper.")

 CHOIR.
. . . IS ONE.

(LIGHTS DOWN.)

END OF THE PLAY

BOW MUSIC

REPRISE: HOW BEAUTIFUL UPON THE MOUNTAIN

PROPERTY LIST

Leonardo's notebook
Table cloth
Seat covers (cloth sheets)
Chalice
Bread and wine
Tableware

NOTE: Leonardo's mural "The Last Supper" should be used as a reference for props and costumes.

Last Supper Scenic Design

1. Bartholomew
2. Little James
3. Andrew
4. Judas
5. Peter
6. John
* Jesus

7. Thomas
8. James
9. Philip
10. Matthew
11. Thaddeus
12. Simon The Zeolot

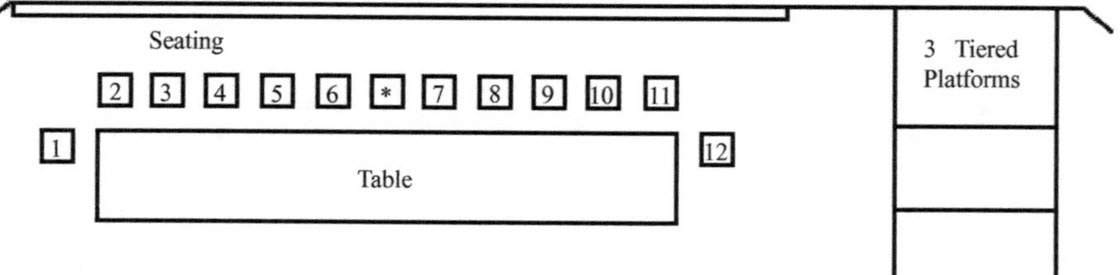

POPULAR MUSICALS
from Samuel French

After the Ball

Avenue X

The Best Little Whorehouse in Texas

The Big Bang

Blood Brothers

Chess

Chicago

Clue: The Musical

Das Barbecü

Eating Raoul

Do Patent Leather Shoes Really Reflect Up?

Doctor! Doctor!

Evelyn and the Polka King

The Gig

Grease

The Green Heart

Gunmetal Blues

The It Girl

It Ain't Nothing But the Blues

James A. Michener's Sayonora

James Joyce's The Dead

Kiss of the Spider Woman

La Cage aux Folles

The Last Session

Leader of the Pack: The Ellie Greenwich Musical

Little Mary Sunshine

Mack & Mabel

Me and My Girl

A New Brain

New York Rock

**AVAILABLE FOR MANY
SAMUEL FRENCH MUSICALS**
Original Cast Recordings on CD
Demo Tapes
Promotional Posters

POPULAR MUSICALS
from Samuel French

The 1940's Radio Hour

No Way to Treat a Lady

Noël and Gertie

Nunsence / Nunsense A-Men!

Opal

Pageant

Pete 'n' Keely

Peter Pan

Phantom

Pippi Longstocking: The Family Musical

Pump Boys and Dinettes

Radio Gals

Return to the Forbidden Planet

Richard O'Brien's The Rocky Horror Show

Ruthless!

Sail Away

Sander's Family Christmas

Scrooge!

The Secret Garden

Shenadoah

Side Show

Smoke on the Mountain

Song of Singapore

The Spitfire Grill

Starmites

Steel Pier

Sweet & Hot: The Songs of Harold Arlen

Swingtime Canteen

They're Playing Our Song

The Wiz

Zombie Prom

**AVAILABLE FOR MANY
SAMUEL FRENCH MUSICALS**
Original Cast Recordings on CD
Demo Tapes
Promotional Posters

ALSO AVAILABLE
from Samuel French

❦❦❦❦❦❦❦❦

Cole
An Entertainment
Based on the Words and Music of
Cole Porter

Devised by
BENNY GREEN & ALAN STRACHAN

Here is a fresh and lively musical about the King of Musicals, Cole Porter. Green and Strachan have cleverly put together most of Cole's hit tunes with a narration which tells the story of his life, from Yale to Paris to Manhattan to Broadway to Hollywood — and, ultimately, back once again to Broadway.

Included are such Porter standards as

I Love Paris
Take Me Back to Manhattan
Love for Sale
Night and Day
I Get a Kick Out of You

A London success, this delightful show may be done very simply on an almost bare stage with projections. The fourteen slides designed for the original London production are available on rental.

5 m., 5 f. (#152)

SAMUELFRENCH.COM

Back to Bacharach and David

THE SONGS OF
BURT BACHARACH AND HAL DAVID

Conceived by
STEVE GUNDERSON
and

KATHY NAJIMY

"Brilliance and silliness."
The New York Times

"Jaunty, bombastic and teasingly lascivious,
it never, ever lets up."
New York Newsday

Songs popular in the 1960s have new life in this glorious collection of hits. At times musically sophisticated, at times brightly satiric, this tribute manages both to celebrate and look back with humor at some of the greatest pop songs ever written. Included are rarely heard gems like "This Empty Place" and "I Just Have to Breathe" and such unforgettable favorites as "Alfie," "Walk on By," "The Look of Love," "Raindrops Keep Fallin' on My Head," "Message to Michael" and "What the World Needs Now Is Love." 1 m., 3 f. (#4314)

Gorilla Man

Book, Music & Lyrics by
Kyle Jarrow

"[Gorilla Man] is big, bloody, ridiculous theatricality...
There's a unity of vision and insanity that's exciting."
--The New York Sun
"Kyle Jarrow's philosophical fable has an antic charm!"
--Variety
"This is a rock musical, and, dare I say it, a great one at
that!"
--Curtain Up
"Kyle Jarrow is New York's hipster playwright."
--The New York Times

Puberty is hard enough without the insatiable thirst for
blood! Waking one morning to find thick fur growing on
the backs of his hands, young Billy discovers the awful
truth his mother has been hiding from him for fourteen
years: he's destined to grow up into a murderous monster.
Cast from his home, he sets out on a journey to find his
father, the legendary Gorilla Man. Combining a variety of
influences including horror films, picaresque tales, and
glam rock, GORILLA MAN is a strikingly original new
musical. It's a pulse-pounding mix of comedy, concert, and
carnival that explores philosophical issues of identity, eth-
ics, and free will. It's a darkly comic coming-of-age tale
filled with bombastic pop songs and peopled with lonely
freaks by Obie Award winning playwright/composer Kyle
Jarrow. (#9929)

"The Big Bang"

Music by
JED FEUER

Book and Lyrics by
BOYD GRAHAM

"World history as a camp musical…. A 'bang'-up sendup of … inspired nonsense."
New York Daily News

"An inventively staged fiesta of eye-rolling idiocy."
Time Out

Performed by its wacky creators Off Broadway, this frenetic entertainment is long on shtick and historical hilarity. It is staged as a backers' audition for an 83.5-million-dollar twelve-hour stage history of the world from creation to the present. Eighteen side-splitting numbers portraying Adam and Eve, Attila the Hun, the building of the pyramids, Julius Caesar and Columbus, among others, give potential investors a taste of the impending extravaganza. In the process, the opulent Park Avenue apartment "borrowed" for the occasion is trashed as the two snatch its furnishing to create makeshift costumes while singing and clowning their way through inventive recreations of the past, stopping occasionally for a little supplicating show biz patter. 2 m. plus on-stage keyboard player. (#4268)